The Dog That Nino Didn't Have

WRITTEN BY EDWARD VAN DE VENDEL

ILLUSTRATED BY ANTON VAN HERTBRUGGEN

TRANSLATED BY LAURA WATKINSON

EERDMANS BOOKS FOR YOUNG READERS

GRAND RAPIDS, MICHIGAN / CAMBRIDGE, U.K.

NINO HAD A DOG THAT HE DIDN'T HAVE.

YES, HE HAD THAT DOG.
EVEN THOUGH HE DIDN'T HAVE IT.

WHEN NINO WENT TO THE WOODS,
THE DOG THAT HE DIDN'T HAVE
DID EVERYTHING THE SQUIRRELS DID.

WHEN NINO WENT TO
HIS GREAT-GRANDMA'S,
THE DOG THAT HE DIDN'T HAVE
DARED TO JUMP ON HER LAP.

WHEN NINO WENT TO THE LAKE,
THE DOG THAT HE DIDN'T HAVE
DOVE STRAIGHT INTO THE DEEP WATER.

THE DOG THAT HE DIDN'T HAVE
HEARD WHATEVER NINO HEARD. ON THE PHONE. WITH DAD.
WHO WAS CALLING FROM A COUNTRY FAR, FAR AWAY.

THE DOG THAT NINO DIDN'T HAVE
LIKED TEARS.
IT LOVED THE TASTE OF SALTY WATER.

NO, MOM DIDN'T SEE THE DOG THAT NINO DIDN'T HAVE.
NO ONE ELSE SAW THE DOG.
ONLY NINO.

BUT SOMETIMES THE DOG ACTED SO CRAZY AND DUMB THAT
PEOPLE STARTED TO NOTICE.

AND SUDDENLY, ONE DAY, NINO DIDN'T HAVE
THE DOG THAT HE DIDN'T HAVE
ANYMORE.

BECAUSE NINO GOT A DOG.
A DIFFERENT DOG.
THIS DOG.
THE DOG THAT HE HAS NOW.

THE DOG THAT NINO HAS NOW IS SOFT.
AND SWEET. AND OBEDIENT.
AND NAUGHTY. AND SMALL.
AND EVERYONE CAN SEE IT.

THE DOG THAT NINO HAS NOW
RUNS AFTER RABBITS IN THE WOODS.
BUT THIS DOG DOESN'T CLIMB THE TREES LIKE A SQUIRREL.

DOES THAT MATTER? OH, NO.

THE DOG THAT NINO HAS NOW DOESN'T LIKE THE LAKE.
BUT IT DOES LIKE DIGGING IN THE SAND. THAT'S FUN TOO.

NINO'S DOG IS SCARED OF GREAT-GRANDMA.
AND DO YOU KNOW WHAT'S FUNNY?
NOW NINO IS TOO.

THE DOG THAT NINO HAS NOW DOESN'T KNOW
WHO DAD IS. HOW COULD IT KNOW? DAD IS SO FAR
AWAY. OR JUST ON THE PHONE. BUT THAT'S OKAY.

THIS DOG MIGHT NOT KNOW SO MUCH
ABOUT DAD AND THE PHONE.
AND IT MIGHT NOT LIKE SALTY WATER.

BUT, REALLY, THAT'S NOT SO BAD.
BECAUSE . . .

BECAUSE TODAY NINO SUDDENLY THOUGHT ABOUT THE DEER.
THE DEER THAT HE DOESN'T HAVE!
AND THE ZEBRA . . .
THE ZEBRA THAT HE'S NEVER SEEN!
AND THE NOT-HIPPOPOTAMUS AND THE NOT-RHINOCEROS,
THE IMAGINARY GIRAFFE,
THE MAKE-BELIEVE BEAR.

AND A FEW MORE DOGS!
DIFFERENT DOGS!
DOGS THAT NINO DOESN'T HAVE!
NINO DOESN'T HAVE ANY OF THEM!
NOT A SINGLE ONE!

Edward van de Vendel has written dozens of books for children and young adults. In 2011 and 2012 he was nominated for the Astrid Lindgren Memorial Award. He lives in the Netherlands. Visit his website at www.edwardvandevendel.com.

Anton Van Hertbruggen has illustrated two critically acclaimed books and has been published in international newspapers and magazines such as *The New York Times* and *The New Yorker*. He lives in Belgium. Visit his website at www.antonvanhertbruggen.com.

First published in the United States in 2015 by
Eerdmans Books for Young Readers,
an imprint of Wm. B. Eerdmans Publishing Co.
2140 Oak Industrial Dr. NE
Grand Rapids, Michigan 49505
P.O. Box 163, Cambridge CB3 9PU U.K.

www.eerdmans.com/youngreaders

Originally published in Belgium in 2013 under the title
Het hondje dat nino niet had
by Uitgeverij De Eenhoorn BVBA
Vlasstraat 17, B-8710 Wielsbeke
www.eenhoorn.be

Text © 2013 Edward van de Vendel
Illustrations © 2013 Anton Van Hertbruggen
© 2013 Uitgeverij De Eenhoorn BVBA
Translation © 2015 Laura Watkinson

Manufactured at Toppan Leefung in China

21 20 19 18 17 16 15   9 8 7 6 5 4 3 2 1

Library of Congress Cataloging-in-Publication Data

Vendel, Edward van de.
[Hondje dat Nino niet had. English]
The dog that Nino didn't have / by Edward van de Vendel;
illustrated by Anton Van Hertbruggen.
pages cm
Originally published: Wielsbeke, Belgium: Uitgeverij de Eenhoorn,
2013, under the title *Het hondje dat Nino niet had.*
Summary: Nino has a wonderful time playing with his imaginary dog
until he gets a real one, and although the new dog does not always
behave as he expects, Nino is still content.
ISBN 978-0-8028-5451-3
[1. Imagination — Fiction. 2. Dogs — Fiction. 3. Pets — Fiction.]
I. Van Hertbruggen, Anton, illustrator. II. Title.
III. Title: Dog that Nino did not have.
PZ7.V556Dog 2015
[E] — dc23
2014048102

Flemish Literature Fund

The translation and production of this book are funded by the Flemish Literature Fund (Vlaams Fonds voor de Letteren – www.flemishliterature.be)